I really enjoyed the simplicity, tone, and pace of the stories. The Scripture references throughout the book not only give support for the ideas on the page but provide a place where a parent can take the child for further study. The discussions at the end of each story pull the main points together nicely. May God bless you as you connect children to Him and give families tools for truth!

Tim Hawks
Senior Pastor, Hill Country Bible Church, NW
Austin, Texas

After reading the stories, I found my spirit stirring throughout the day as I was challenged to apply God's two great commandments to my own life. I can't tell you how powerful the stories were for me! I love the brilliant and creative ways you illustrate God's purpose to a child!

Joanna
Benbrook, Texas

I was touched by the inner workings of this precious child's heart. His questions share a message of the eternally-existent, perfect, almighty Being, the Creator of heaven and earth. When you give this beautifully written book with stunning illustrations to your child, you will give a gift that lasts forever.

Carolyn Hargrove
Second Grade Teacher, River Place Elementary
Austin, Texas

"God's Spirit in the Heart of Every Child" presents profound spiritual truths in language that is simple and enjoyable enough for a child. The Scriptures intertwined within the text reinforce that these are not just cute bedtime stories but eternal truths that can change the hearts of the next generation.

Sharon Gardner
Hospital Chaplain and Author
Leander, Texas

The stories and the illustrations are both exceptional. They have a strong spiritual and practical message so badly needed today. God bless you for your eagerness to spread God's word.

     Father George Von Kaenel
     Glenrock, Wyoming

How wonderful these stories are. They really ministered to me as right now the teenage woes are upon us, and I want our son to be a little boy again so badly. It occurs to me that the messages you have put in these books are timeless, and they will be great gifts to parents and their children at all ages. I love how the stories flow together and how deep the stories are YET still on a child's level of understanding. I'm amazed by your ability to communicate with the written word.

     Selina
     San Antonio, Texas

Desmond says: "My God book Dad, read it again, read it again!" and "What's that?"' pointing to the light emanating from the children's hearts. I say, "What is that Desmond?" He says "yight" and giggles raising his shirt. I can't wait to buy my friends a copy. Really.

     Jon
     Austin, Texas

God's Spirit in the Heart of Every Child

Timeless Short Stories

Michele Zink Harris

Illustrated by Don Collins

Next
Generation
Hearts

A note from the author

Our children are growing up in exciting and uncertain times. My prayer as a parent is to help equip our three boys with a spiritual wisdom to match their intellectual creativity—and then to get out of the way. The goal of these short stories is to unite our world through the spirit of God's two Great Commandments, and the hope in our children's hearts.

Please join me in celebrating the way, the truth, and the life of the next generation. Theirs is a potential limited only by their ability to align with the dreams of God, the love of Christ, and the power of the Holy Spirit.

Endless possibilities indeed. Michele

A note of appreciation to illustrator Don Collins and graphic designer Brad Grulke, for bringing my vision to life, and to my husband Dave, for never holding me back. Words cannot express my gratitude and love for you.

Biblical reference: The New International Version, ©1995 The Zondervan Corporation

For more information, please contact Michele at michele@nextgenerationhearts.org and find additional resources at www.nextgenerationhearts.org.

Dedication

To A.J., Kyle, and Joshua. God's greatest gifts and my greatest teachers.

I'm Looking for God

I couldn't find Him
in my dictionary

the Truth

Jesus answered, "I am the Way and the Truth and the Life..." **John 14:6**

One day I was looking for God. I went to the obvious place to find things…my dictionary…and to my surprise God was not in there.

I began to look in the places where other people say they find God. I looked in the churches and the chapels. I looked under the seats and behind the door. I looked under the altar and behind the statues.

I looked everywhere out there. I could not find Him.

I began to look in the heavens where other people say they find God. I looked at the sun and the moon. I looked at the planets and the stars.

I looked everywhere out there. I still could not find Him.

I began to look in nature where other people say they find God. I went to the mountains and the desert. I went to the forest and the sea. I traveled miles and miles. I looked everywhere out there. I simply could not find Him anywhere!

I became sad and frustrated. "He is not out there!" I cried. "He simply is not there. I cannot find God out there anywhere! I am not looking out there any longer!"

Then I began to think. "If God is not out there, then He must be somewhere else. But where else is there?" I wondered. "If He is not outside me, could God be inside?"

Instead of looking for God out there in the world where things are so busy and noisy and confusing…

I began to look for Him inside me where it can be quiet and still. I gave myself some time and listened carefully with my heart instead of struggling with my head.

Be still, and
know that I am God.
Psalm 46:10

I realized that is exactly where He is. God's spirit is inside me!

Once I realized God's spirit is inside me, I realized God's spirit is inside YOU!...and YOU!...and YOU!...and YOU!

...nor will people say, "Here it is," "There it is," because the Kingdom of God is within you.
Luke 17:21

Even if YOU haven't realized it yet!

Then the most amazing thing happened. I began to see God's hand everywhere! God's spirit is in the churches and the chapels. God's hand crafted the sun, the moon, the planets, and the stars. God's hand created the mountains, the desert, the forest, and the sea. God's hand painted the sunrise and the sunset.

God's spirit is present in every loving, joyful, humble, compassionate, forgiving, peaceful act of the world.

God created us in His image, each unique, but equal in His eyes.

...now you are light in the Lord.
Live as children of light.
Ephesians 5:8

God's image is in me and God's image is in you!

Knowing God's spirit is in all of us connects us in a special way. Knowing we are all created in God's image makes it easier to be fair and honest, kind and respectful.

...with God all things are possible.
Matthew 19:26

Knowing God loves all of us reminds us that we have everything we need.

Now I find God's hand everywhere and in everything!
And I know you can find God too.

Jesus said, "I am the light of the world. Whoever follows me will never walk in darkness, but will have the light of life."
John 8:12

You just have to know where to look first.

Story inspired by A.J. Harris, age 6.

Story Discussion
The Greatest Commandments

Love the Lord your God with all your heart and with all your soul and with all your mind. This is the first and greatest commandment.
Matthew 22:37-38

God created the heavens and the earth and everything in it. (Genesis 1:1) We must remember that God specifically created us in "His image." (Genesis 1:26-27) The first of the two greatest commandments calls us to get to know God our Creator. Three important ways we can get to know Him are through His word (the Bible), through His walk (the life of Jesus), and through His whisper (the Holy Spirit).

And the second is like it: Love your neighbor as yourself.
Matthew 22:39

Once you realize you are created in God's image and you spend time understanding His word and His walk, then you will begin to see His image in other people. When we can do this, it is easier to love, and to encourage, to respect, and to care for each other. We also can see God's hand more easily in all creation.

God, What Should I Be When I Grow Up?

A story of God's gifts and His spirit within us

the Life

Jesus answered, "I am the Way and the Truth and the Life…" **John 14:6**

"Daddy, how do I know what God wants me to be when I grow up?" I believe God wants you to use the gifts He gave you.

"What gifts are those?" When God created you, He gave you special gifts. He wants you to use your special gifts to glorify what He has created in you.

"How do I know what my gifts are? How will I know the special gifts that God wants me to use?" You will know them because to each of these gifts God has attached the Bird of Inspiration. "The Bird of Inspiration! How in the world will I know what that is?" I exclaimed.

You will know you are using the special gifts God gave you when you feel the qualities of the Bird of Inspiration that He has attached to each one. "What will I feel, Daddy?"

The Bird of Inspiration has a heart that soars with passion. God has given you a deep desire to do certain things. Follow your passion. The Bird of Inspiration has a set of strong wings that persevere. Not everyone will see your gifts as important, or as worthwhile, or as special as you do. Do not give up. Persevere through this.

There are different kinds of gifts, but the same Spirit.
1 Corinthians 12:4

The Bird of Inspiration has a soul that sings with praise. When you are using your gifts, you will feel happy, satisfied, and complete. Remember to sing praise to God for blessing you with these gifts.

"Wow! Do I have just one of these special gifts? Do I have just one of these wonderful Birds of Inspiration to find?" Oh, no, dear child of mine. God has given you many to find. Throughout your whole life you will find different Birds of Inspiration to enjoy.

You may be inspired to work with your hands to paint, to build, to sculpt.

You may be inspired to work closely with others to teach, to heal, to parent. You may be inspired to work to figure out new things, to research, to develop, to write.

Whatever you do, work at it with all your heart, as working for the Lord, not for men.
Colossians 3:23

Your gifts may be numerous, and they are unique to you. That is why God has attached the Bird of Inspiration to them, so you will know the special gifts when you find them.

"Thank You, God! Thank You for these special gifts and for the Bird of Inspiration to help guide me," I sang.

The Bird has another quality that is important for you to remember. "What is that, Daddy?" The Bird of Inspiration is free. "What exactly is freedom?" I asked.

I believe: Freedom is knowing that God created you. Freedom is knowing that God is the only one you need to impress. Freedom is knowing that God is impressed by anything you do with a heart of peace, love, and compassion.

Jesus said, "Then you will know the truth, and the truth will set you free."
John 8:32

Don Collins

God truly loves you, my child. He made you to be free.

God does not command that we do great things, only little things with great love.
Mother Teresa

The Bird of Inspiration was inspired by Carlyn Nelson.

Story Discussion
The Greatest Commandments

Love the Lord your God with all your heart and with all your soul and with all your mind. This is the first and greatest commandment.
Matthew 22:37–38

Keeping all parts of yourself fixed on God your Creator is the surest way of finding those special gifts that He has given you to use through your life. If you love God with all your heart, your passion will be clear. If you love God with all your mind, He will give you the strength to persevere. If you love God with all your soul, you will never forget to turn back to Him with praise.

And the second is like it: Love your neighbor as yourself.
Matthew 22:39

Realizing your gifts is only part of God's plan. Using your special gifts to benefit all God's people completes the joy and freedom He has planned for your life.

Each one should use whatever gift he has received to serve others...
1 Peter 4:10

Spiritual Gifts Reference
1 Corinthians 12:4–11

There are different kinds of gifts, but the same Spirit.

1 Corinthians 12:4

For we are God's workmanship, created in Christ Jesus to do good works, which God prepared in advance for us to do.

Ephesians 2:10

We must always remember we are "God's workmanship." He created us exactly as we are supposed to be with exactly the purpose He intended. The Bird of Inspiration is an analogy of God's Holy Spirit. The Bible tells us that different gifts are given to each of us through the Holy Spirit to be used for a specific God-given purpose, and for the common good of all people. So enjoy your gifts and sing praise back to the Giver of everything!

...where the Spirit of the Lord is, there is freedom.

2 Corinthians 3:17

What Makes God Smile Makes Us Strong

*Allowing God
to work through us*

the Way

Jesus answered, "I am the Way and the Truth and the Life..." **John 14:6**

"Mommy, I want to know what it is that makes God smile."
I would love to teach you what I believe makes God smile.
When God smiles the world is a better place because His
hand is more fully seen in it. "What is it that I need to do?"
It takes more than simply 'doing' certain things. It also
requires that you 'give up' certain things to God as well.

"What are the things I need to give up? I didn't think there was
anything God needed from me." God needs you to have a
pure heart when you do things in His name. Because of this,
there are things you need to give up to be free to do the things
that make God smile.

"Mommy, what do I need to do to have a pure heart?" Come to God when you are sorry for the things you have done wrong. He forgives you. Then you must also forgive yourself by surrendering to Him all your shame and guilt about what you have done. Remember that God created you just the way you are to do His good works upon the earth. Shame and guilt simply get in the way.

Blessed are the pure in heart, for they will see God.
Matthew 5:8

"Lord, I will give You all my shame and guilt."

There is no place for judgment toward another. Give all your judgmental thoughts to God. It makes God smile when He sees love and respect among His different children. Remember, ALL are created in God's image. We are equal in His eyes.

This is My command: Love each other.
John 15:17

"Lord, I will give You all my judgmental thoughts."

There is no place for fear and dishonesty. Give all your fear to God. Always be courageous even when you feel afraid to tell the truth. Remember, when you are honest, God will be right there by your side. *"Lord, I will give You all my fear."*

But whoever lives by the truth comes into the light, so that it may be seen plainly that what he has done has been done through God.
John 3:21

There is no place for anger, blame, or aggression toward another. Surrender all your blame and anger to God. It makes God smile when you are patient and kind toward one another. Remember to forgive each other just as He forgives you.

"Lord, I will give You all my anger and blame."

There is no place for worry and doubt about what you can do. Give all your concerns to God. It makes God smile when you trust Him completely. Remember, God has placed you here for a special purpose. *"Lord, I will give You all my doubt."*

...to be rich in good deeds, and to be generous and willing to share.
1 Timothy 6:18

There is no place for greed. When you feel you do not have enough, surrender this to God. It makes God smile when you are generous and compassionate toward one another. Remember, He will supply all your needs. *"Lord, I will give You all my greed."*

There is no place for jealousy. Give all your desires to God. It makes God smile when you are grateful for your blessings and encourage one another. Remember, life is not a competition. Do not be jealous of another's gifts, but glorify God by using your own. *"Lord, I will give You all my jealous desires."*

There is no room for God in a person that is full of himself.
Baal Shem Tov

There is no place for pride. Your talents are gifts from God, so surrender your pride. It makes God smile when you are humble and turn your worship and thankfulness to Him. *"Lord, I will give You all my pride."*

You see, my child, when we surrender to God the parts of ourselves that separate us from Him, we are completely open to have God work through us. His spirit strengthens us. His spirit strengthens the whole world.

I can do everything through Him who gives me strength.
Philippians 4:13

So neither he who plants nor he who waters is anything, but only God, who makes things grow.
1 Corinthians 3:7

Can you imagine how strong the world would be if every child allowed God to work through them in this way?
God can.

Story Discussion
The Greatest Commandments

Love the Lord your God with all your heart and with all your soul and with all your mind. This is the first and greatest commandment.
Matthew 22:37–38

The greatest of God's laws is all about surrender. Jesus was the perfect example of surrender to God's plan. Don't think of this as giving up or giving in when you are trying something new or playing a game with a friend. But rather think of throwing away all the useless stuff that separates you from having a pure heart and truly knowing God—your shame, your doubt, your fear, your anger, your pride. Remember God created you, so He knows you better than anyone else. He wants more than anything for you to trust Him for everything.

And the second is like it: Love your neighbor as yourself.
Matthew 22:39

Something miraculous happens when you know God is walking with you as you work and play. You will begin to see God's image in the people around you. God's will about how He wants us to treat one another and His plan for our lives become clear.

Jesus answered, "I am the Way and the Truth and the Life…"
John 14:6